Wild Tales

Wild Tales

ADAM PFEFFER

iUniverse, Inc.
Bloomington

Wild Tales

iUniverse books may be ordered through booksellers or by contacting:

iUniverse
1663 Liberty Drive
Bloomington, IN 47403
www.iuniverse.com
1-800-Authors (1-800-288-4677)

ISBN: 978-1-4759-5386-2 (sc)
ISBN: 978-1-4759-5387-9 (e)

Printed in the United States of America

iUniverse rev. date: 9/28/2012

Books by Adam Pfeffer
Published by iUniverse:

KOLAK OF THE WEREBEASTS

TWILIGHT OF THE GODS

THE MISSING LINK

TO CHANGE THE WORLD and OTHER STORIES

THE DAY THE DREAM CAME TRUE and OTHER POEMS

THE VISITORS

THE CREATION OF GOD

THE AMAZING SLICK MCKINLEY:
GREATEST ATHLETE EVER

THE FANTASTIC FLYING MAN

THE GENIUS WITH THE 225 IQ

30 GREAT STORIES FOR OUR CENTURY

WILD TALES

Contents

The fashion of the day is usually at the cleaners tomorrow.
BUDDY "BOOGIE" ROCKET

Smarty Pants

---

*T*here was a man who took off his pants one day and the pants walked away. The man immediately called the pants, Smarty Pants.

Smarty Pants kept walking no matter what the man called him. He walked down the hallway and was greeted by Mrs. Cumblebun.

"Hello there," she said, as the brown Smarty Pants walked past her with nobody inside.

Of course, Smarty Pants did not answer back.

"Well, that's a good how do you do," Mrs. Cumblebun exclaimed. "Nobody even says, hello, anymore."

Smarty Pants kept walking. He walked past Mrs. Cumblebun and went down the stairs. He almost bumped into Mr. Pogler.

"Everybody's in such a hurry these days," mumbled Mr. Pogler, very annoyed. "Why don't you watch where you're going, young man?"

But there was no young man inside Smarty Pants, and so, he kept walking away.

"You'd think they would at least say excuse me," grumbled Mr. Pogler. "More than you can expect these days."

Smarty Pants, without saying a word, kept walking. He waited at the door of the apartment building until someone came along and opened it. Smarty Pants then walked onto the sidewalks of the city.

Just because there was no one inside the brown pair of pants didn't really matter to anyone in the big, noisy city. People hurried on their way to all kinds of places and Smarty Pants kept walking to somewhere.

He walked two blocks and then someone shoved him from behind. "Look out, young man, I'm in a hurry," someone said.

Smarty Pants moved to the right and let the person pass. "Some people are so slow," the person mumbled. "It really is annoying."

Smarty Pants kept walking. He walked among the crowd of people in the big, noisy city and no one noticed that a pair of pants was walking without anybody inside.

"Hi, honey, don't you look sharp today," said a woman standing outside one of the stores. Smarty Pants stopped for a moment, made a sort of bow, and then kept walking.

As he made his way past one store, a little dog began barking. Smarty Pants began to walk faster. The dog kept barking, following the pants down the street. Smarty Pants began to run. The dog began running and barking after him.

People began to stop what they were doing and watched what was happening. "Is that a pair of pants being chased by a little dog?" asked a man standing nearby. "What will they think of next?"

The children began to laugh, pointing at the pair of pants running down the street being chased by the little dog. Parents frowned, telling their children that this was an example of living in the big, noisy city. The children continued to laugh.

Smarty Pants continued to run from the little dog. He ran through the crowd of people without a sound. Eventually, the little dog caught him. He growled and bit at the pants leg and began pulling Smarty Pants to the ground. Smarty Pants did not say a word. He did not say a word because no one was inside.

"That dog is hurting that young man," some woman was saying. "Somebody better call the cops."

So they all called the cops and a police officer walking nearby answered the call. He walked right over to where the little dog was pulling on Smarty Pants and told the little dog to stop. The little dog let go of Smarty Pants and ran back to its owner, who was standing in front of one of the stores.

"Are you all right, mister?" the police officer asked Smarty Pants. Smarty Pants did not answer. "You want me to call an ambulance?" the police officer asked Smarty Pants. Smarty Pants did not answer.

A crowd of people began to gather around Smarty Pants. "Who is he?" asked someone in the crowd. "I've never seen him before."

Smarty Pants got down on one knee and the police officer told everyone to stay back. "This is an emergency," the police officer said. "This man is injured."

So the police officer called an ambulance and the people watched in horror as Smarty Pants fell to both knees. "He's really in very bad shape," a woman in the crowd said. "That poor young man."

When the ambulance finally came, they put Smarty Pants on a stretcher, and took him to a nearby hospital.

"Don't worry, sir, everything's going to be all right," they told Smarty Pants.

When they arrived at the hospital, they brought Smarty Pants inside. "It doesn't look good," one of the hospital attendants said. "Bring him to emergency."

"Name please?" one of the hospital workers asked. Smarty Pants did not answer.

"He's in bad shape," the worker said. "I don't think he's well enough to give me the information."

They marked his chart, "John Doe," and then brought him to an examination room. "A doctor will be with you very shortly, sir," the hospital worker said. "Please remain calm."

Smarty Pants sat down in one of the chairs and waited. One of his pant legs had been ripped by the little dog. He sat with his legs crossed hoping no one would notice the small tear.

"Hello, Mr. Doe," the doctor said, stepping into the room. "How are you feeling?"

Smarty Pants did not answer.

"Can you talk?" the doctor asked.

Smarty Pants said nothing.

Then the doctor began examining the torn pair of pants. "There's nobody inside," he finally said. "Is this some kind of joke or something?"

Smarty Pants did not reply.

"This hospital is for people who are really hurt," complained the doctor. "Not for a torn pair of pants with nobody inside."

So they took the pair of pants and put them outside in the dumpster where the garbage was kept. An old man, who had no money, spotted them as he was walking by.

"They look nice," he said to himself. "I'll try them on."

When the old man bent down to grab the pants, Smarty Pants stood up and began to run away. "I need a drink," the old man said. "Maybe I've had one too many."

Smarty Pants ran down the sidewalk of the big, noisy city. He ran and he ran and nobody did anything to stop him. In fact, he wasn't even really noticed among the crowds of the big, noisy city.

The dogs noticed him, however. They all barked and Smarty Pants kept running. He finally collided with a woman carrying her groceries. The woman screamed. Smarty Pants bowed, the creases showing in the sunlight, and then began to run onward.

"Stop that man!" the woman screamed.

But no one stopped Smarty Pants as he kept running down the sidewalk. He finally reached an apartment door, and when somebody opened it, Smarty Pants darted inside.

Inside one of the apartments, a man was walking around without his pants on. Smarty Pants walked into his room and the man smiled.

"Ah, there you are, Smarty Pants," the man said.

Smarty Pants did not reply.

The man reached down and put Smarty Pants on. "Seems like you're a little torn," the man muttered. "I'll have to have you fixed."

Smarty Pants did not say a word, but the man smiling, put on his coat and was about to leave the apartment, when Smarty Pants suddenly fell down. Before the man knew what was happening, Smarty Pants took off for the door.

"Hey, come back!" shouted the man.

Smarty Pants, however, didn't come back. He opened the door, kept running, and was never seen by the man again.

He eventually went into business, became very rich, and married a quite beautiful white silk gown.

The Day of Peace

---

*E*veryone was fighting and arguing so much, a day of peace was declared around the world.

At the United Nations, it was decided there would be peace for one day throughout the world on a Wednesday in May. Countries fighting, arguing, or just plain not getting along, were told they would have to stop what they were doing and be pleasant to one another. There would be no exceptions.

Many leaders when told of the declaration said they would spend the day in bed. "We'll let the armies of the world sleep late, and then we'll all have tea, coffee, or a nice glass of milk," one leader explained.

Although some countries were opposed to having a day of peace, the leader of the United Nations told the world that he would not give in, and that there would be peace on that Wednesday in May.

Everyone hoped it would be a beautiful day, and any talk of rain was forbidden. "There will be peace, and it will be beautiful and sunny," declared the leader of the United Nations.

Schools were declared closed for the day, and the shopping malls told to stay open late.

"Now we'll finally see what the world is like when there is total peace," said the leader of the United Nations. "Anyone caught fighting or arguing will be taken off to jail."

There was much talk of the big day with people thinking of all the things they would do. It was sure to be the greatest of all holidays.

When the day arrived, people woke up early to hurry outside to see what a day of peace would be like. They were met by police officers, who ordered them back to bed.

"Everyone must stay in bed and sleep late!" one of the officers said. "You are ordered to enjoy yourselves on this day of peace!"

Little Tootie Hopper heard the officer, and smiled. She went back inside her house with a shake of her head. "Isn't there more to peace than just sleeping?" she asked her mother.

"Don't worry, I'm sure there will be some fun things to do," her mother replied. "They just want everyone to be peaceful and well-rested."

Sure enough, before Tootie could fall back asleep, she heard music playing outside her window. She leaped out of bed, and ran to the window. It looked like a parade was marching down the street!

Tootie and her friends were soon outside. It was a parade, a long line of people wearing various costumes playing drums and trombones and trumpets marching down the street accompanied by a group of clowns, acrobats, and dancers!

People were handing out hot dogs, hamburgers, and ice cream to everyone free of charge.

"Enjoy this day of peace," someone was saying. "Everyone is ordered to treat each other with kindness on this beautiful, sunny day!"

And all around the world, people stopped fighting and arguing. All the different armies of every nation were ordered to stay in bed, and then, after being served a good breakfast, were allowed to attend the parades. Yes, there were parades all over the world!

Then the amusement parks were opened, and everyone was allowed in without paying. Little Tootie Hopper and her friends rode the roller coasters, the space ride, and all the other rides until they were so tired, they had to sit down and catch their breath.

Food at the amusement parks was also free, and everyone spent the day eating cotton candy, ice cream, and hot dogs. Tootie alone ate two ice cream cones and three hot dogs!

"This is the best day of the year!" she shouted. "Hooray for peace!"

And peace there was. Not one person fought or argued with his or her neighbor. People were friendly and kind to each other. And when they saw a person struggling with a package or two, they immediately ran to help.

In anticipation of the day, people had sent packages of food and medical supplies to all the starving and less fortunate people of the world. On the day of peace, the packages were opened and the food was handed out.

"We hope everyone can enjoy their meal with music and dancing," said the leader of the United Nations. "Then everyone will really know what peace is like."

Because the armies of the world were no longer fighting, people celebrated with huge feasts. In England, Italy, Greece, Germany, Denmark, Russia, China, Japan, and most of the other countries of the world, there was dancing, singing, foods of all kinds, and pastries in various shapes, such as stars and half-moons.

In the United States, little Tootie's mother invented something she called a "Blue Sky Pie." It was an open pie filled with blueberries and sweet cream with marshmallow clouds topped with whipped cream.

"This represents the blue sky of peace," Tootie's mother said, presenting it to the mayor of the city. "It's sweet, and yet, good for you."

After the mayor said a few words, everyone made their way to the nearby park. A huge stage had been set up, and when the park became filled with hundreds of people, musical bands began taking their turns singing songs of peace and good will. People stayed in the park even after the sun went down, and many danced and sang along with the groups on stage.

And you know something? The same thing was happening in every city and town across the United States! There were songs and dancing and everyone felt free and happy.

That is, all except Old Man Bitterman. He growled and snarled most of the time, grumbling that things were better in the old days. "Why, we had peace parades that used to last for days," he said. But it really wasn't true, of course. But even Old Man Bitterman smiled when he was given a slice of "Blue Sky Pie."

After the concert was over, a huge fireworks show lit up the night sky. Little Tootie stood there with her mother and father, and watched as the fireworks exploded in the darkness. Peaceful music accompanied the show, and then when it was over, everyone went home.

"I hope everyone enjoyed themselves during this special day of peace," the president said on the television. "The people of the world certainly deserved it."

The next morning, Tootie woke up early and could hear the cars honking their horns again and the people shouting at one another. "If only there could be a day of peace every day," she said. Then she slid out of bed, and ran to her mother and father.

"I can't wait until next year!" she said. "That was the greatest holiday ever!"

Amanda Panda

---

*A*manda Panda, she loves her bamboo.
She sits in the zoo and chews on it day after day.

But Amanda Panda is unhappy because she's stuck in the zoo. "I'd really like to see the city," she would say to herself almost every day.

"I'd like to take a taxi or a bus and go shopping the whole day! I'd visit every store in the city until I got just what I wanted.

"When the hours finally passed away, I'd go to see a show. A delightful musical play.

"When it was over, I would stand and applaud and wish that it went on forever!

"Then I would invite all my friends from the zoo over for tea. We'd laugh and we'd talk and then we would all agree, there was nothing better than to see the city and be free! Oh, yes, so very free!"

As Amanda Panda thought all this, she would chew on a stick of bamboo. And then she would look around at all the cages and pits and sigh.

"I'd like to go out and look for a dress," she would say to herself. "A beautiful dress, fit for a queen!

"Then I'd buy great big jewels and try them on one at a time. They would sparkle and glow on my fingers and arms, and then I would put a big, twinkling necklace on and smile like a princess. Oh, everyone would be so surprised because they had never seen a panda like me!

"Then I'd get my hair done. Maybe I'd wear it in a big bun or maybe in a long braid. But when I finally decided and everything was taken care of, everyone would say how beautiful I looked. More beautiful than the emperor's wife!

"After that was finished, I'd go back out on the town and watch all the people hurrying off to all the different places they go to. Where do they go to in such a hurry? Well, I would like to see!"

As Amanda Panda thought this last thought, she became very sad. She nibbled on another stick of bamboo, carefully pulling out the tender shoot, and thought once again.

"I guess if I was in the city, looking at all the people," she thought. "The people would also look at me.

"They would think that I was a wild animal, looking to hurt all the little children.

"They would call the police and run away shouting that an animal had escaped from the zoo! They wouldn't know that I only wanted to see the people rushing around and maybe play with the children.

"But how would they know what I really wanted to do? I'm not very good with words because I didn't go to school. And they would run away before I could explain and return with people who wanted to chase me down.

"Yes, they would chase me and then set a trap!

"And when I was finally caught, lying in a big net, they would all gather around me and clap and shout and laugh that I was caught!"

Amanda Panda kept on chewing on her stick of bamboo, and then began to think new thoughts.

"I haven't any money," she said to herself. "Though I don't really know what it's used for.

"And I haven't any clothes. Though I don't really know what I need them for.

"And I can't think of a reason to wear ribbons and bows and big, sparkling jewels.

"And as much as I like the theater, the people would all be staring at me while I watched the show.

"They'd wonder why a panda wanted to be free."

Amanda Panda rolled on her back, still chewing on the bamboo.

"And maybe they're right," she finally decided. "I really don't have a need to fight and argue with anyone.

"I have no need for money, and well, here at the zoo they do feed me regularly.

"And if I did go out, and suddenly it began to rain, who would bring me inside so I could stay nice and dry?

"You know, I really don't like to complain. But it really wouldn't be very nice getting wet."

Amanda Panda grabbed another stick of bamboo, and smiled.

"Maybe I'm happier than I thought," she said to herself. "Maybe it's really not so bad being in the zoo. Except for the bars and the cages.

"But I can always sleep when I like, and I can roll around on the grass and eat my bamboo all day long. And at night, I can look up at the stars and think about the twinkling lights.

"And I can always talk to the tigers, the lions, or the sheep. They understand me, and well, it's fun telling stories to each other."

Amanda Panda began to grin.

"No, it really isn't all that bad," she said to herself. "I'd like to be free, but this is my home, and everyone leaves me alone. And the people aren't afraid of me here, not even the little children.

"No, the children are friendly to me here."

Amanda Panda, she loves her bamboo.

She sits in the zoo and chews on it day after day.

And now Amanda Panda is happy because she's decided she really is safer in the zoo. She sits and watches the children, and they sit and watch her.

And that's the way it should be, she smiles to herself.

The Tree Hugger

There was a girl known as The Tree Hugger. She loved Nature so much, she went around hugging all of the trees that grew upon the land.

"Hello, mighty oak," she would say, greeting the tall trees. "I love you so much I will give you a great, big hug."

And that's exactly what she did. She walked up to a thick tree, put her arms around the trunk and stood there hugging it for quite a while. She really didn't know whether the tree enjoyed itself because, as everybody knows, trees can't talk.

But when she walked away from the big tree, she felt much better about giving her love to Nature.

"Hello, weeping willow," she said, greeting the drooping tree. "I love you so much I will give you a great, big hug."

And she began hugging the willow tree with as much affection as she could muster.

"It's so nice loving all of you," she said to the trees of the forest. "I want to hug each and every one of you."

And that's exactly what she did.

One day, she was busy hugging an old oak tree when she suddenly heard a noise. It sounded like breathing.

She looked up at the old oak tree and noticed that somehow it had opened its eyes. Yes, that's right, this old oak tree had eyes, the color of coal, on its upper trunk.

"You're alive," The Tree Hugger said with great surprise.

The Tree Hugger looked at the old oak tree and saw a mouth appear underneath the coal-black eyes.

"Yes, of course, I'm alive," said the old oak. "Your nice demonstration of love and affection has awakened me from my sleep."

The old oak tree then smiled.

"Wow, I never talked to one of you before," The Tree Hugger said. "But this is the best thing that could ever have happened."

"I hope you still think so after conversing for a few minutes," said the old oak. "You see, I'm plenty upset about all of my friends being knocked over."

The Tree Hugger thought the old oak tree had a pleasant voice. It sounded like a sunny day in May, The Tree Hugger decided.

"I'm trying to stop your friends from being knocked over," explained The Tree Hugger, "but it's not easy."

"Why do the Stick-Legs hate us?" the old oak tree asked.

"Oh, you mean the human beings," The Tree Hugger said.

"Human beings?"

"Yes, that's what we call ourselves."

"Funny name for a Stick-Leg," the old oak tree grumbled. "Well, why do they insist on buzzing through our bodies?"

"Well, they make things out of your wood," The Tree Hugger explained.

"May they rot with termites," the old oak tree said.

"They don't know you're alive," The Tree Hugger said.

"Well, how do we grow if we're not alive," the old oak tree wanted to know.

"They think you're just plants."

"Plants? But we are the hard people."

"The hard people?"

"Yes, that's what we call ourselves," the old oak tree explained. "And we pray to the sun and the wind throughout our lives."

"You probably know a lot about Nature," The Tree Hugger said.

"Nature?"

"Yes, you know the wind and the hills and the birds and the sky--"

"Oh, you mean the light paths," the old oak tree said.

"The light paths?"

"Yes, all the beings and things that are paths for light and sun and knowledge."

"But how were human beings supposed to know?" The Tree Hugger asked.

"You destroy that which you don't know?" the old oak tree asked.

"Yes, that is the way with the Stick-Legs."

"I wondered if that was not a rock on top of their bodies," the old oak tree said.

The Tree Hugger laughed.

"My rock thinks of the hard people and those of the light paths," she said.

"That is good and holy," the old oak tree said. "You will be influenced by the light of the sun and will know the ways of all beings."

The Tree Hugger smiled.

"Yes, that's what I was hoping for," she said. "I knew the hard people were something special."

The old oak tree smiled and then reached up with one of his narrow tree limbs and came down holding an acorn.

"This is our seed," he said. "The wind and the rain make sure more of us grow from the earth."

"Yes, and your breath adds life to the wind and the air," The Tree Hugger said.

"Yes, you are wise," the old oak tree said. "Take this and may you be a path for the light."

The old oak tree handed The Tree Hugger the acorn. The Tree Hugger held the acorn in her hand and then threw it into the wind.

"May you grow and look up to the light," she said as she threw the acorn. "May you live and add many more seeds to the earth."

The old oak tree smiled.

"Yes, you are a good one, young Stick-Leg," he said. "Tell your people that the earth needs the hard people and those of the light paths to keep the earth alive."

The Tree Hugger nodded her head. "I've known for a long time," she said. "If I can only make them listen."

"You will make them listen," the old oak tree said. "They must know that if the hard people and the beings of the light paths should leave forever, the earth is sure to die."

"Some Stick-Legs don't want to know," she said.

"You must explain to them they will find out a bitter truth if they do not listen."

The Tree Hugger smiled and then put her arms around the old oak tree. "I will not fail," she whispered to the old oak.

The wind answered with a warm breeze as she stood there hugging the old tree.

Cat McCool

There's a cat in orange shorts
hanging out at the pool.
Everyone knows him as
Cool Cat McCool.

The dogs never bark
when he comes walking around,
Not even Old Jake,
the grumpy bloodhound.

The birds fly away
when Cat McCool comes close,
They know he's as quick
as a high leaping ghost.

The cats all love him,
The Persian,
The Tabby,
The Manx,
and the Siamese.

When Cat McCool walks the streets,
he does what he pleases.

The mice run away,
They know they're in danger.
They don't want to know him,
To them he's a stranger.

The people all laugh,
The boys,
The girls,
Mothers,
And old men,
To them he's Cat McCool
an honorary citizen.

Once in the alley,
a cat did pick a fight,
He cornered Cat McCool,
And told him he'd bite.

But Cat McCool stood his ground,
he hissed and showed his claws,
The other cat snarled and he spat,
And then Cat McCool landed a paw to his jaw.

The cat ran away,
Cat McCool was hailed as a hero,
He now had no enemies,
They all counted zero.

So he walked around
with his head in the air.

And was given a medal
by the town mayor.

And when he finally went home,
kicking a can,
He opened the door,
and saw Mary Ann.

Did he throw out his chest,
and try to scratch her boot?
Did he hiss and snarl
like a wild galoot?

No, Cat McCool purred
and then made a leap
into her arms
like a kindly tame sheep.

For you see it was so,
very much a fact,
Cat McCool was simply
Mary Ann's cat.

"And how was your day,
my frisky young dear?
I'm glad that you finally
made it back here."

Then she held up his paws,
and said with a laugh,
"Cool Cat McCool
you do need a bath!"

So the brave Cat McCool,
what did he do?
He jumped out of her arms,
and leaped into the pool!

And everyone knows him as
Cool Cat McCool!

Snoozer Smith

We call him Snoozer Smith because all he does is sleep. After a whole night of sleeping, he sleeps at the breakfast table. When the buses come and take him to school, he sleeps in class. At lunch, he sleeps in the cafeteria. After school, he comes home and goes right to bed. He sleeps more than the cat!

Now I ask you, isn't that someone who should be called, Snoozer Smith?

I should know because you see Snoozer Smith is my little brother.

Snoozer Smith, why do you sleep all the time?

He just looks up, shrugs his shoulders, and puts his head back on the kitchen table.

WHY DO YOU SLEEP ALL THE TIME?

"It's the Sandman's fault," he finally says.

"Then you should find him and talk to him," I reply. "Anything but sleep all the time!"

He looks up and smiles at me. "That's exactly what I'm going to do," he finally tells me. "I'm going to find that Sandman and tell him to stop throwing all that magic sand in my eyes."

"You'd better do it now," I tell him.

"Why is that?" he mumbles.

"Because you're about to fall asleep again!" I finally shout at him.

He picks his head up off the kitchen table and smiles again. "Not this time," he says to me very seriously. "This time I'm going to find him before I fall asleep."

Then he stands up and begins looking for the Sandman. I think what he really needs to do is go to the doctor, but I don't say that, and let him go on looking for this Sandman character. Where do you look for the Sandman, anyway?

But my little brother, Snoozer Smith, says he knows where to find the Sandman. So he begins looking. He looks in the cookie jar because he says sprinkles look like sand. Can you believe it? It turns out it was just an excuse to eat a cookie before dinnertime.

Now where do you look for the Sandman, anyway?

"I know," he says, finishing off the cookie. "In the bedroom, of course."

Sounds reasonable to me. So the two of us go up the stairs and look in his bedroom. No Sandman.

"Maybe he's hiding under the bed," he says, suddenly yawning.

We look under the bed, but there's no sandman hiding there. In fact, there's no sign of the Sandman anywhere in his bedroom.

"I'll find him," he says, yawning again.

He is yawning so much, he's got me tired. So then I begin yawning. All I want to do is sit down in a chair and rest. I look over at Snoozer Smith and he's crawling on top of the blanket of his bed.

But what about the Sandman?

There's no time for the Sandman because we're both yawning away. And then I watch as Snoozer Smith lay down on his pillow still yawning. I'm about to close my eyes when I see a little man with a white pointed beard walk through the wall of the bedroom. He's totally dressed in dark blue with two white boots and a pointed hat on his head. Yep, it's the Sandman for sure. I see he's carrying in one hand a small sack of sand, and he's preparing to dip the other hand in and take out some magic sleeping sand, when I open up my eyes and shout.

"It's him!" I scream. "The Sandman!"

I didn't mean to scare him too badly, but when I shouted he was so stunned he dropped his small sack of sand on the floor.

"Now I got you," I say to him. "You can wake up now, Snoozer Smith, we have found the Sandman."

I look over to my little brother as his head is flying off the pillow. "The Sandman!" he shouts. "I knew I would find you!"

The little white-haired man is still standing there not saying a word. Then I turn to him, very upset, and shout at him.

"Out with it!" I say to him. "Why do you make Snoozer Smith fall asleep all the time?"

He looks at me and then at Snoozer and he smiles.

"Aw, it's all a big joke to you, isn't it?" Snoozer says.

This changes the expression on the Sandman's face. He is no longer smiling.

"Now I assure you," he says in a dreamy voice, stepping forward. "Snoozer here is one of my best customers. There's nothing I wouldn't do to give him a nice, peaceful sleep."

"But why do you make him sleep so much?" I ask him.

"Well, you see," he starts saying in that dreamy voice of his, "every time someone yawns, it echoes through the air and I'm alerted. It's my job to stop the yawning and make you fall asleep."

"But what about Snoozer Smith?"

"Well, Snoozer," he says with a sheepish grin, "Snoozer Smith as you call him, well, he yawns more than anybody in the world. As I said, he's my best customer."

"So every time he yawns, you put him to sleep?" I ask him.

"Yes, I guess you could say that," he tells me. "But you see it isn't just putting you to sleep that I do. Oh no, this magic sand I carry with me does more than just put you to sleep. You see, the great thing about this sand I use is that it brings on the most pleasant of dreams.

Dreams of all sorts. Why we make thousands of dreams every day down at the Dream factory."

"Dream factory?"

"Oh, yes, why your dream last night that you were the greatest football player who ever lived was created especially for you at the Dream factory," he says, bending down to pick up his small sack of sand.

"Then you must be working overtime for Snoozer's dreams," I say to him.

The Sandman smiled. "We enjoy making pleasant dreams for everyone," he says. "Why, someday I'll take you to Slumberland and show you exactly what I mean."

The whole explanation was getting me a little tired. I began yawning and then realized what was going on.

"Here comes the Sandman," I heard him say as I felt a handful of magic sand hit me in the eyes.

When I opened my eyes again, the Sandman was gone. I tried looking for him everywhere, but no such luck. Then I see my little brother wake up from his sleep and sit up on the bed.

"The Sandman's gone," I tell him.

He just shrugs his shoulders and rolls out of bed smiling. "Yeah, but I ain't going to yawn too much anymore," he says.

I smile, but before I know it, Snoozer's yawning again.

"Well, here comes the Sandman," I say.

Snoozer shrugs his shoulders, and jumps back onto the bed. He's ready for another nap.

And that's why we call him, Snoozer Smith!

Little Little B. Little

———————————

L ittle Little B. Little was very little. He was as big as your hand standing up and that's pretty little if you ask me. Everything he owned was little.

He had a little car. He had a little house. He had a little dog. He had a little wife.

His wife was so little, she could fit in your hand without any trouble. She was a good wife, though, which made little Little B. Little very happy if only for a little while. For you see, before too long, the Littles began to fight. No one could really hear them, but they began to shout at each other.

It all began because little Little B. Little refused to put on his gloves. His wife, whose name was little Lillian B. Little, was very upset. She knew what would happen if her husband came down with a cold. Oh, well, she refused to even think of it.

Little Little B. Little didn't care at all. He didn't remember the last time he was sick and had to stay inside for a week, coughing and sneezing and getting everyone else, including the little dog, very sick.

"You put on those gloves!" shouted little Lillian B. Little.

"Why should I put on gloves when I'm not cold!" shouted back little Little B. Little.

"Because if you don't put on gloves you will be cold!" shouted little Lillian B. Little.

Little Little B. Little would not listen. He was a little stubborn if you ask me.

So he went outside without his gloves and it was so cold and windy, little Little B. Little came back coughing and sneezing. Yes, he had gotten a cold.

Little Lillian B. Little was furious. "I told you what would happen if you went outside without your gloves!" she shouted.

"Right as always, my dear," little Little B. Little managed to say in between coughing and sneezing.

The words brought a smile to little Lillian B. Little's face. "So now you know I was right," she said. "Well, in that case, I will take care of you until you get better. But you better listen to me next time, mister."

Little Little B. Little nodded his head and then got into his little bed. His little dog curled up beside him.

"Little Spot B. Little, it's nice to have you by my side," he said to the little dog. "But you better get out of here before you get sick."

The little dog didn't pay any attention to little Little B. Little's words. He continued to lay at his side.

"Okay, but don't blame me if you get sick," said little Little B. Little.

Little Lillian B. Little then walked into the room carrying a little bowl of soup. She had a little spoon sitting beside the little bowl.

"Eat this and you will feel better," she said.

So little Little B. Little ate the soup from the little bowl with a slurp and a swoosh. He finished it with the little spoon and decided that he was beginning to feel a little better.

"Maybe I'll do a little reading," he said to himself. "That should make me feel a little better."

So he read a little book about a little family living in a little town and he smiled a little smile.

Little Lillian B. Little came into the room and sat down beside him on the little bed. She had a little smile on her face as she saw what her little husband was reading.

"How are you feeling?" she asked her little husband.

"A little better," he said with a little sneeze.

"You'll feel even better tomorrow," she replied. "All you need is a little night's rest."

So Lillian B. Little took the little book and gave little Little B. Little a little kiss on the forehead and then shuffled out of the room. Little Little B. Little smiled and then he put his head on his little pillow and fell fast asleep.

He dreamed a little dream about a little dragon and how he convinced the little dragon to leave the little castle because he was frightening everyone. You see the little dragon didn't understand that the little people were afraid of him. He thought he was the same as them. Little Little B. Little laughed as he explained to the little dragon that he was quite different from the little people.

"You even eat the little people sometimes," he said.

"No, not me," the little dragon replied. "I don't eat anything that has two eyes and moves about on the land."

"Is that so?" said little Little B. Little. "Then what do you eat?"

The little dragon smiled and told him that he ate the little flowers that grew among the little trees.

"That's not scary at all," said little Little B. Little. "It's really a little funny."

"Yes, now you understand," said the little dragon. "I'm not trying to scare anyone. That's not the kind of dragon I am."

"Well, I never heard of a nice dragon before," said little Little B. Little. "But I'll explain everything to the little people."

And he did. And the little people were a little happy to hear that the little dragon was not mean or cruel. And that's when little Little B. Little woke up in his little bed.

"I feel a little normal today," he told little Lillian B. Little. "I think I will go outside."

"Wear your gloves," said his little wife.

"But I'm not cold," he replied.

"You saw what happened the last time you didn't listen," his little wife warned him.

"That was the last time," he said. "Now I think things are a little different."

"Well, don't ask me to take care of you if you get sick again!" little Lillian B. Little shouted. "That's going to be a little different, too."

So little Little B. Little went outside without the gloves and what do you think happened?

He came back coughing and sneezing, of course.

"I warned you," little Lillian B. Little said.

"But I told you things were a little different," said little Little B. Little.

"And how are things different?" his little wife wanted to know.

"This time the dog is sick, too."

Yes, that's right, little Spot B. Little was coughing and sneezing, too.

"Well, I'm not going to take care of you," said little Lillian B. Little.

"But we need you, my dear."

Then it happened. Little Lillian B. Little began to cough and sneeze, too. "Now we're all sick," she said.

So little Little B. Little and little Lillian B. Little and little Spot B. Little all climbed into the little bed.

"What we need is a little sleep," said little Little B. Little. "And maybe dream a little dream."

But when he looked at his little wife and his little dog, they were already sleeping. So little Little B. Little rolled over onto his little pillow and fell fast asleep. Soon, he was talking to the little dragon again about the little yellow flowers that grew near the little trees on the little hillside.

Jangles: Santa's Sheepdog

One snowy Christmas while Santa was out,
Delivering presents to children, no doubt.
He went down the chimney, if only he'd known,
A litter of puppies there all alone.

"Hello, madam, how do you do?"
He said to the mother sheepdog he hardly knew,
"Are these your little ones here all around?"
But she looked at him cautiously and did not make a sound.

"Perhaps, I can help you," said a little girl from behind.
"These are my puppies, Santa, if you don't mind."
"Beautiful creatures," he said with a jolly old laugh.
"And I'll leave them all presents on your behalf."

"Santa, these puppies here were just born.
And I'm making sure they stay safe and warm.
But maybe you'd like a present one time.
Something to cheer you in the springtime."

Santa smiled at her and thought,
"Not a bad idea, maybe I ought.

"But which one of these Christmas babies should I take?"
"Maybe the one who's eating your cake!"

He looked down, and sure enough, one white and blue,
"Is eating the cake I left there for you!"
Santa laughed at the little girl's news,
Then the little dog stumbled, and fell on his shoes.

"He's ringing the bells attached to my boots!
I'll call him, Jangles, it's a name that he suits."
Then he reached down and patted the little girl's head,
"I'll take him next Christmas!" is all that he said.

Then he gave the little girl her gift,
And went up the chimney in one mighty lift.
"Ho, Ho, Ho," she could hear Santa say.
"I'll come back for you, Jangles, on Christmas Day!"

Now Santa thought about the little cute pup,
And told Mrs. Claus when the evening was up.
"Darling young child, she wants you to smile."
"Why, I'll give her a present of the very best style!"

"Then the pup will be ours, it's settled and done,
And I'll take him on journeys, and there will be fun."
And he kissed Mrs. Claus so tender and true,
And waited for Christmas when the puppy was due.

And that Christmas, Santa found the house once again,
He slid down the chimney with a gift for young Gwen.
"Oh, Santa, you've returned, just as you said.
And here is the puppy waiting for your sled!"

Santa looked down at the big pup at his feet,
And said, "Jangles, my friend, at last that we meet."
The white and blue sheepdog sat up with a bark,
And gave Santa his paw as if he were smart.

Santa laughed and put out his hand,
And the sight of the two of them was something grand.
"I hope he can see with that hair in his eyes."
"He can, dear old Santa, though no one knows why."

Then they laughed and they laughed, and he gave Gwen a coat.
And she put it on with a lump in her throat.
"Oh, Santa, it's beautiful!" she said with a sigh.
And then they began saying to each a goodbye.

"Goodbye Santa! Goodbye Jangles, too!"
And up the chimney together they flew.
And when Jangles saw the reindeer crowd,
He sniffed, and he panted, and barked very loud.

Now Santa saw the reindeer stayed true,
It was sheepdog talk, a language they knew.
And so when Jangles jumped into the sleigh,
Santa shouted to the reindeer, "Up, up and away!"

And then the snow drifted down from the gray-colored clouds.
And Jangles sat next to Santa barking aloud.
This kept Santa's reindeer alert and spry,
And with Rudolph's red nose, they sped through the sky.

With Jangles still barking, the birds flew away fast,
And nothing could keep Santa from completing his task.
He completed his journey around the world that night,
And headed back to the North Pole with the first morning light.

"Thank heavens, you made it," Mrs. Claus said with a shout.
And she spotted Jangles, his tongue hanging out.
"What a beautiful sheepdog!" she said with a smile.
And Jangles answered with a bark, as they landed meanwhile.

"He was born on Christmas!" Santa said with a laugh.
"But I think that he's tired and could use a bath."
"I think that we'll wait," Mrs. Claus nodded her head.
"For I see the young one has just gone to bed."

And, sure enough, there in the sleigh,
Was Jangles curled up and snoring away!
"I guess it really has been a long night,
And Jangles was busy all through the long flight."

So they carried him into Santa's warm home,
And Mrs. Claus tucked him in with a bone.
And they slept very well that very first night,
And Jangles was the first one to wake with the light.

He sniffed and he pawed and soon was outside.
And he sat in the sleigh waiting to ride.
"Not today, Jangles," Santa said with a laugh.
"Christmas is over and spring's coming fast."

And the year went by, it seemed like a flash,
And Christmas was coming again in a dash.
Jangles played with the reindeer and elves,
And Santa now counted it would soon be month twelve.

So they finished the toys and packed them away,
To give to the children with which they would play.
And Jangles helped much of the year,
And Santa was pleased to have Jangles near.

And Christmas was coming as they all knew it would,
And Santa finished his list of all who were good.
And on Christmas Eve, Santa took flight.
With Jangles, the reindeer, and a dark winter's night.

With Rudolph's nose shining, up the sleigh flew,
Jangles was barking what the reindeer should do.
And Santa was jolly, as jolly could be.
He climbed down the chimneys, and left gifts by the tree.

And as they were flying, Jangles started to bark,
And Santa knew there was something there in the dark.
So he steered the sleigh down to the ground far below,
And there was a poor cat stuck in the snow.

"What are you doing out here so late?"
But the cat could not answer it had made a mistake.
Santa reached down and pulled him out of the drift,
Then gave him some catnip as a Christmas Eve gift.

The cat was quite happy and then ran away,
And Santa was laughing and up went the sleigh.
And soon they came to Jangles' old home,
And Gwen was waiting with a brand new comb.

"And how are you, Jangles?" she said with a smile.
And Santa gave her a gift, and they talked for a while.
Then a sheepdog came into the room at last,
And Jangles was wagging his tail so fast.

And Jangles licked his mother with glee,
And a tear fell down Santa's cheek to his knee.
And Gwen remarked how Jangles did grow,
And before they knew it, it was time to go.

"Goodbye, dear friends," Santa did say.
"And maybe we'll return on a hot summer's day."
Wagging his tail, Jangles just barked,
And then went up the chimney to return to the dark.

They finished their work by morning's new light,
And returned to the North Pole where they ended their flight.
Mrs. Claus was waiting there with a smile,
And she patted Jangles' head and Santa laughed all the while.

"Our work is done for another year," Santa said.
And then Jangles dashed off to the house, right to bed.
And that spring, Jangles found an injured reindeer in the woods.
And Santa was happy and knew Jangles was good.

They brought the young reindeer back to the yard,
And Santa helped heal him, and Jangles stood guard.
"He just might be one of my reindeer some day."
And Santa laughed while the reindeer did play.

And all that summer, Jangles and the reindeer did romp,
And when work was to be done, Jangles was prompt.
"You're a good sheepdog," Santa said with a roar.
"I'm glad you'll be with me this Christmas once more."

And soon the autumn winds they did blow,
And the elves kept on working, the pile of toys it did grow.
And when it was close to Christmas at last,
They loaded the sleigh and heard the forecast.

"Snow and fog," the weatherman said.
And Santa hooked up the reindeer and Jangles jumped in the sled.
And now on this Christmas, Santa was sure,
With Rudolph and Jangles, the team would endure.

And as they flew through the sky, Santa did say,
"Merry Christmas to all, and a very good day!
Happy Christmas, my friends, peace on earth.
Good cheer to all, and to all much mirth!"

With a shout and a laugh, they vanished from sight,
And all one could hear in the dark night,
Was Jangles the sheepdog barking on and off,
"Merry Christmas to all, ARF! ARF! ARF! ARF!"

The Leprechaun O'Doon

*I*t was St. Patrick's Day and Nora and Sean rushed through the dark green fields of Ireland searching for a leprechaun. They knew leprechauns were the fairy shoemakers who were said to possess a pot of gold and knew where all the wealth of the world was buried, and St. Patrick's Day was the best time of the year to find them.

They kept running and searching, but still there was no sign of the tiny men. "Oh, Sean, where do you think they're hiding?" asked Nora, looking under a nearby rock. "But I really thought today would be our best chance to be lucky."

"All we have to do is keep searching," Sean replied. "We're bound to catch one eventually."

After a while, they got tired and sat down to rest on a couple of large rocks. That was when Nora spotted the large field of clover growing on the side of a green hill. "Oh, look, Sean," she said. "All we have to do is find a four-leaf clover and then we'll surely attract a leprechaun."

Sean nodded. "Yes, holding a four-leaf clover," he said, "is said to make them appear with their pot of gold."

They dashed to the field of clover, and began looking for one with four leaves. Ah, but a four-leaf clover is not so easy to find. Nora and Sean finally realized that after searching through the field.

"All I see is three-leaf clovers," sighed Nora. "There must be at least one four-leaf clover in this whole field."

They kept searching and searching, until finally they decided they would never find a four-leaf clover. "It's no use," Nora said with a sigh. "I don't think we would find one if we searched forever--"

It was at that moment Nora looked down and spotted something shimmering among the clover. She bent down, and sure enough, there among all the three-leaf clovers was one with four leaves.

"I can't believe it," she shouted. "Right there underneath my nose."

Sean ran over to Nora as she began pulling the four-leaf clover out of the ground. As she pulled it up, they spotted a tiny man in a bottle-green suit and green pointed hat resting underneath.

"A leprechaun at last!" Sean said, grabbing the little man by his green jacket. "So that's where you've been hiding."

"'Tis true, 'tis true," said the leprechaun. "Now what would you be wanting from me?"

"Why your pot of gold, of course," Sean said. "Now that we've caught you, don't you have to show us where it is?"

"All true," said the leprechaun. "Except I'm only an apprentice leprechaun. The name's Finnegan, at your service."

"Well, Finnegan, where's the pot of gold?" Sean demanded.

"Well, you see, sir, I have no pot of gold of me own," he said. "But I'll take both of you to O'Doon and he'll surely reward you kindly."

"Don't take your eyes off him, Sean," Nora said. "If you do, he'll vanish for sure."

"'Tis true, 'tis true," Finnegan agreed with a nod of his head. "But I will be taking you to O'Doon, anyway."

They followed the little ten-inch man to the top of the hill. "O'Doon will be here any minute," Finnegan said. "He always appears on St. Patrick's Day."

They waited for a few moments, and then Nora began to get angry. "This is just another one of your tricks, isn't it, Finnegan?" she said.

"No, no, me dearie, O'Doon already knows you're here."

"How could he know that?" Sean asked.

Finnegan smiled. "We leprechauns know a lot of things," he said. "More than you human beings will ever realize."

Nora frowned, and just then, a tiny leprechaun wearing a bottle-green suit and a green hat with a feather in it sitting atop a beautiful white horse with a twisted horn in the middle of his forehead appeared before them.

"Wow!" Nora and Sean both gasped at the sight of him. "Why, that's a unicorn!"

"Yes, 'tis true," Finnegan said. "And now, my little friends, I would like to introduce you to O'Doon."

"Please to meet you, sir," Nora said. "We are in great need of your pot of gold."

"Yes, I know all about it," said the leprechaun on top of the unicorn. "But, you see, I can't give you any of me pot of gold if it is only for yourselves."

"What do you mean?" Sean said, looking up at the tiny man. "We need that gold for our family."

"But there are lots of families who be needing me gold," O'Doon said. "Why should I be giving it to you?"

Nora stared up at the tiny leprechaun and saw that he had a red beard and gleaming sliver buckles on each of his shining leather shoes. "But we're the ones who found you," she finally said. "And today is my birthday."

"Ah, a St. Paddy's child," O'Doon said with a smile. "But the only way I be parting with me gold is if both of you promise me that you'll not be using the gold just for yourselves, but to help others who are also in need."

Nora looked at Sean, and they both nodded their heads. "Yes, of course," Nora said. "We'll help as many families as we can." She then walked over and gave the four-leaf clover to O'Doon.

O'Doon smiled. "Sure is a pretty piece of greenery," he said, holding the four-leaf clover. "Now you two climb up here on Clover's back and I'll be taking you to the end of the rainbow."

"The end of the rainbow?" they both repeated.

"Ay, that's where me pot of gold lies," O'Doon replied.

Nora and Sean climbed up onto the unicorn's back, holding onto O'Doon, and they galloped and flew through the air over the hills of Ireland. After a while, they began to see colors appear in the sky. They were all the colors they had ever seen and they floated next to each other in a huge arc.

"The rainbow is very beautiful," Nora said, holding tight to O'Doon.

"Yes, me lovelies, the most beautiful part of the old country," he said. "And there, down below, is me pot of gold."

The unicorn soared through the sky, and then they floated upon a gentle wind, along the arc of the rainbow. As they got close to the end, bright patches of sunlight began to appear.

When Clover the Unicorn landed, Nora and Sean could see many tiny leprechauns guarding a huge black pot of gleaming golden coins. They watched as O'Doon waved to the tiny men, and then they were helped off the unicorn. As O'Doon slid off the shining white unicorn, he walked over to the pot of gold and began to smile.

"You see, me lovelies, this be me pot of gold," he said, still holding the four-leaf clover Nora had given to him. "But since today be your birthday, I'll be giving you something better than a few gold coins. Instead, I'll be giving you this small leather purse. As long as you own it, it will never run out of gold coins. Now, remember your promise to help others and then we be sending you on your way back to your home and family."

Nora and Sean took the small leather purse, and before they knew it, they were back in their own village. They immediately gave some of the gold coins to their parents, and then when more appeared, they gave them to everyone in the village. The coins never ran out and they lived happily ever after.

Old Man Winter and
the Four Seasons

---

*O*ld Man Winter comes blowing into town in the middle of December.

One blast of breath freezes up everything!

Why, before too long, the pond is frozen solid, and the water in the air begins to crystallize, falling to earth as white, blinding snow.

When Old Man Winter gets to chattering, a wicked wind gushes through the streets. It's a wind that chills the bones and makes you talk in cold puffs of air.

And he sticks around for a while. I mean, there's nothing you can do to make him go away.

When he gets angry, you'd better run or take cover inside a nice, warm house. I remember one time he got so angry that snow was falling for two days! Yes, and a chilling wind whipped that snow into huge piles. It got so bad, people had a hard time driving and all the schools were closed.

Every time Old Man Winter gets angry, they call it a blizzard. And, sure enough, that's exactly what it is. A blizzard of snow and wind and temperatures so cold, it makes your nose numb.

To some, Old Man Winter's not so bad. His bursts of anger and chattering bring the snow that some people love to play in. Why, there's skiing and skating and building forts and snowmen.

The problem is Old Man Winter stays too long. He doesn't even think of leaving until the end of March. And there's nothing you can say to make him leave before that time.

It's at the end of March that Old Man Winter finally goes away and allows his daughter, Young Maiden Spring, to take over. Well, that's one of the nicest things Old Man Winter ever does.

Young Maid Spring is a pretty one, I'll tell you that. And she loves her flowers!

When she sees what her father, Old Man Winter, has done to the land, she usually begins to cry. She cries a lot in the beginning, and the rain comes pouring down washing away the snow and the ice left behind by Old Man Winter.

She's a nice one, too. Why, she's as nice as Old Man Winter is mean. It doesn't even seem as if they're related.

When Young Maid Spring starts chattering, it's a warm breeze that blows and all the birds and animals sometimes chatter back. Because she's so nice and kind, the birds and animals are not afraid to let their young ones walk around, and see the world for the first time.

And because of all her crying, sending the rain falling to the earth, the flowers begin to bloom. Well, I told you, she loves her flowers. When she's through cleaning up the land, thousands of flowers grow! In all sorts of colors: blue, yellow, red, and white!

She also loves the trees. When she sees what Old Man Winter has done to them, she cries at first. Then something magical happens. The trees grow back their leaves, and the land is green and beautiful once more!

The problem is Young Maid Spring doesn't stay long enough. While no one is sad when Old Man Winter leaves, they are sorry to see Young Maid Spring fly away. But fly away she does, and that's because it's time for her mother, Madam Summer, to take over.

Madam Summer isn't as mean as her husband, Old Man Winter, but when she gets going, it gets mighty hot around here.

It must be from living with Old Man Winter because Madam Summer likes it hot. And when she starts shouting, well, it could scare your pants off! They must have some arguments because the thunderstorms they produce are filled with crackling lightning and booming thunder.

I don't know what Old Man Winter shouts at her, but it rains pretty hard. Madam Summer must be crying at something the old geezer said.

When it finally stops raining, it's hot and sweaty once again around here. She must be constantly turning up the heat being with that old stinker, Old Man Winter.

She's definitely not as mean as her husband, I can tell you that. Why, when she makes it hot, it's fun to go to the beach or the swimming pool, and just jump in and feel totally refreshed. It's definitely more pleasant than a blast of her husband's frigid breath.

Then, in August, Madam Summer lets the dogs out, and everything becomes hot and lazy. I guess that's why they call it "the dog days of summer."

Anyway, by the end of September, Madam Summer has had enough and she lets her rowdy son, Wild Man Autumn, take over. Boy, is he a handful! He's almost as bad as his father, Old Man Winter. A real chip off the old block, if you ask me.

The first thing Wild Man Autumn does is make sure everything is ripe. He does this so everything will start falling out of the trees. Then he makes the farmers reap the fields until everything is dead or dying. Although it will all come back to life when Young Maid Spring returns, he doesn't care.

Then Wild Man Autumn goes after the trees. He starts coloring the leaves, and because of this, they begin falling off the trees!

Yes, a real wild one, if you ask me. Then, if that's not enough, the noisy stinker begins to howl. The wind he creates blows the leaves all over the place, and anything else that's not nailed down. Boy, when he starts having one of his fits, it looks as if the world is coming to an end.

But, you know, there are some people who like Wild Man Autumn. They actually enjoy all the colors he paints the leaves, and when they fall off the trees, they like playing in huge piles of them. That is, until the little stinker begins howling again, and blows the leaves across the yard.

After going wild and painting everything in sight in orange, red, and brown, the colors begin to dim. Soon everything turns to a hazy shade of gray. It must be because he's Old Man Winter's son!

Just like his old man, Wild Man Autumn begins to blow cold winds through the streets. It's appropriate he's in charge when Halloween comes around. He becomes as scary and spooky as an old witch!

All the howling and cold wind sure gets things ready for Old Man Winter. And when the land is finally bare, Wild Man Autumn takes off and leaves everything for his father to begin the year again.

And so, things change from one thing to another all because of that family, the Four Seasons. They're a wacky, wild clan, I can tell you that. But they've been around for years, and I don't think they're leaving anytime soon!

Whatchamacallit

---

*T*hey placed the furry little creature down on the table. It squeaked and then it barked like a little dog.

"What did you say it was?" one of them asked.

"A whatchamacallit," Bobby Driscoll replied.

"Never seen one before," somebody else said.

"Do they bite?" little Lisa Henry wanted to know.

"They have teeth," Bobby Driscoll answered, "but they're small and hidden by a long tongue."

Lisa put her hand out and touched the little creature.

"His fur is very soft," she said with a smile. "Why does he have all those whiskers?"

"Must need them for some reason," somebody said.

"Is it a boy or a girl?" Lisa Henry asked.

Some of the other children standing there giggled.

"Beats the heck out of me," Bobby Driscoll replied. "I guess we'll just have to see if it has babies in the next few weeks."

"Oh, can we have one?" Joey Baum asked, shaking his arms.

"Can't really say right now," Bobby Driscoll said. "We'll have to wait and see."

They stood there watching the little creature when it suddenly picked up its little furry head and opened its tiny mouth.

"Squeak," the creature said.

Everybody started laughing until the little creature began to whistle like a tiny bird.

"Maybe he knows how to sing," Joey Baum said.

"A little ditty from a whatchamacallit," Lisa Henry laughed.

They all watched as the whatchamacallit stood up on its little legs and began to dance. It was a little dance with the little creature moving its little legs back and forth.

"You better name him Fred Astaire," one of the adults said.

But the whatchamacallit wasn't finished. It began whistling a tune, a very lively tune, and dancing at the same time.

"Hollywood, here we come," Bobby Driscoll laughed.

The whatchamacallit kept dancing and whistling until it suddenly stopped and began squeaking once again.

"Show's over," Lisa Henry said. "You were great, Fred."

"Wow, he was pretty good," Joey Baum said with a smile. "Think you can get him to do that in front of a whole audience of people?"

"I don't see why not," Bobby Driscoll said. "All you have to do is feed him some gobbledygook."

"That's what he eats?" Lisa Henry asked.

"That's all he eats."

Bobby Driscoll bent down with some gobbledygook in his hand and fed it to Fred the whatcamacallit.

Fred ate it very quickly and began squeaking once again.

"Here we go again."

The whatchamacallit began dancing and whistling just as he had before. Everyone laughed and applauded.

When the whatchamacallit was finished, he stopped, squeaked, and became very quiet.

"I'll put it on the internet," Joey Baum said. "I have a video of the whole thing."

And so, Fred the whatchamacallit was put on the internet and became a national sensation.

When everyone was invited back to Bobby Driscoll's house, there was a surprise. There on the table was Fred the whatchamacallit and a little black creature with antennae and two large hind legs.

"What is it?" Joey Baum asked.

"Well, you all know Fred and this is a thingamabob," Bobby Driscoll explained.

"Well, what does he do?" Lisa Henry wanted to know.

"Just watch."

Bobby Driscoll then fed both the whatchamacallit and the thingamabob. The two creatures touched each other and then the entertainment began.

While Fred the whatchamacallit danced and whistled, the thingamabob twirled and leaped. He leaped over Fred and he leaped into the air. Bobby Driscoll then took out something red from his pocket and placed it on the table.

"This is a whirligig," he said. "He completes the act."

The red whirligig began spinning like a top as the thingamabob leaped up over them and Fred the whatchamacallit whistled and danced. Everyone was amazed.

"I call the thingamabob Gizmo and the whirligig Doohickey," Bobby Driscoll said. "We're going to call the act, The Rigamaroles."

Everyone laughed and applauded.

The Rigamaroles became very famous and performed their little act throughout the world. They would still be performing except for the fact that Bobby Driscoll ran out of gobbledygook somewhere near Kansas City. Without gobbledygook, Fred, Gizmo and Doohickey refused to do anything but just sit and be very quiet.

Bobby Driscoll brought them home one day and they just slept and slept. They continued to sleep until Bobby Driscoll finally had more gobbledygook delivered from Podunk, wherever that is.

But it wasn't the same anymore. Even with a new supply of gobbledygook, the Rigamaroles refused to perform.

"That's show biz," Bobby Driscoll said with a sigh. "The only thing to do is to find new doodads and dojiggers."

He did just that and then went out and bought a huge supply of gobbledygook, but none of the creatures he brought back ever performed like Fred Astaire the whatchamacallit, Gizmo the thingamabob and Doohickey the whirligig.

Abra Cadabra

Abra Cadabra was the most superstitious person I've ever met. Yeah, that was his name, Abra Cadabra. I met him one summer walking around in the fields near my home. He was a normal looking kid, but I could see right away that there was something different about him.

"What are you doing?" I asked him, spotting him picking up something from the grass.

"Found a four-leaf clover," he told me.

"Wow, they're pretty rare," I replied.

"Don't talk for another 30 seconds or the magic will wear off," he said with a finger at his mouth.

"Never heard that one before," I said, apologizing for saying something.

"If you talk, the clover fairies will hear you and they won't let you make a wish," he said.

"Clover fairies?"

"Yeah, they're all over the place and if you find one of their four-leaf clovers, they have to grant you a wish," he explained.

I watched as he made a wish over the four-leaf clover.

"Guess you'll be rich very soon," I said with a smile.

"Oh, I didn't wish for money," he said. "I wished for a magic wand."

I smiled, and then I saw him frowning.

"Oh, no, I told you my wish," he groaned. "I'd better say a prayer and hope that the fairies still grant my wish."

"You could just apologize," I said.

"No, this calls for something more drastic," he told me.

Then he took out what appeared to be a cracked marble and began rubbing it in his two hands.

"What the heck is that?" I asked.

"A boiled marble," he said. "They're very good for bringing back magic to a wish."

"You think the fairies know about it?" I asked with a smile.

"Oh, yes, boiled marbles are very popular beyond the rainbow," he said very seriously.

I didn't know whether to laugh or run away from him. I mean, this kid was talking about fairies and beyond the rainbow as if they really existed. Next thing you know he would tell me that pigs could fly.

"Hey, where do you live?" I asked him.

"Beyond the rainbow, of course," he replied.

I smiled.

"And your mother is Mother Nature, right?"

He looked surprised. "Yes, how did you know?"

"How did I know? Am I supposed to laugh?"

"Not if you want the fairies to be offended," he said.

I couldn't believe this kid. I didn't know whether he was being serious or he was off his rocker.

"Who's your father?" I asked.

"Father Time, of course," he answered.

"Oh, right, your mother is Mother Nature and your father is Father Time. And your brother and sister are Dawn and Dusk."

He looked quite surprised. "Yes, that's true, of course."

"I don't believe it," I gasped.

"You'd better tap your foot," he told me. "That's the only way you'll be able to hear the truth."

"Tap my foot?"

"Yes, when someone says they don't believe, they have to tap their foot in order to hear the truth," he explained.

"Is everyone beyond the rainbow as superstitious as you?" I asked.

He frowned. "I don't know what you're talking about," he said. "It isn't superstitious, it's perfectly reasonable logic."

I wanted to laugh. "Yeah, boiled marbles do sound pretty reasonable," I said.

"Yes, and I'll give you one so that you may make a wish," he said.

He pulled out a marble from his pocket and handed it to me.

"What do I do?" I asked.

"You rub it on your shirt and then make your plea to the fairy world to hear your wish," he said.

"Okay, I'm game," I said.

So I rubbed the boiled marble on my shirt and made a wish.

"Don't tell me what you wished for," he said with a smile.

"Okay, I won't," I said. "But if it comes true, then I promise to believe everything you said."

"Oh, it will come true all right," he said. "That is if you don't step on any lines going home."

"Oh, I won't," I assured him.

It suddenly became very windy. He looked at me very seriously and put up his hand.

"I have to be leaving now," he said. "That's my uncle coming to take me home."

"What? The wind is your uncle?"

"Yeah, that's right."

And before I could say another word, a strong gust lifted him right into the air and sent him sailing over the hills.

"Wow, he might have been telling the truth," I said to myself. "No, but how?"

I thought about Abra Cadabra all the way home. I decided I wouldn't tell anyone about him. No one would believe me or they would think I was crazy or something. A child of Mother Nature and Father Time. No, there was no way I would ever tell someone that.

When I got to my house, I saw something sparkling in the late afternoon sun. No, but it couldn't be. Yes, it was there all right. A brand new blue bicycle sitting by the stairs. It was what I wished for with the boiled marble Abra Cadabra gave to me.

"Oh, no, but it can't be," I said.

Then I began tapping my foot. I looked at the bicycle and knew that my wish had really come true.

"Thanks everyone!" I began shouting into the sky. "Thanks so much!"

I later found out it was my parents who bought me the new bicycle. Not fairies, not Mother Nature, not Father Time.

"Who do you think bought you the bike?" my father asked.

"Oh, you're not going to believe it," I said.

That night, I sat in bed rubbing the boiled marble on my shirt. I wished for something, smiled, and then fell asleep.

In the morning, I ran downstairs and heard the barking. "Our new puppy!" I said laughing.

"Yes, we just bought it," my father told me.

"Bought it? But I wished for it last night," I explained.

"He wished for it," my father laughed.

"Try buying something with a wish," my mother said.

I put the boiled marble in a drawer and haven't made any wishes in quite a while. It was just too spooky for me. Everything came true but not in the way I expected. Meanwhile, I never saw Abra Cadabra again. But when it's very windy and the sun is sinking down, I think I hear him shouting in the sky. I would never tell anyone that, of course. Who would believe it?

The Day It Rained Cats and Dogs

Black clouds spilled in from the north, settling over the little town of Oakmont. Everyone rushed to get home before the huge storm began.

"This is going to be a whopper," old Johnny Blake was saying to anyone who would listen. "Why, this is going to be a storm just like they had in the good old days."

The weathermen had already predicted it was going to be one of the worst storms of the year. And so, as people hurried to finish their shopping and work before the storm began, there was a huge crash of thunder.

"Here we go," laughed old Johnny Blake. "Just like the old days."

But after the thunder, no rain fell.

There was another sudden crash of thunder and then an echoing blast of lightning and then a black cat with a white stripe fell from the blackened sky. No one in Oakmont seemed to notice. They were busy waiting for the rain to come pouring down.

"Where's the rain?" everyone wondered.

"Oh, it will be coming down in no time at all," they were assured.

Then there was another crash of thunder and a bolt of lightning, and a small white poodle fell from the sky. He landed with a thud and then ran off barking through the streets.

The black clouds grumbled and then several cats, black, white and tan, came falling from the sky. Several dogs followed. The dogs were of different breeds and as they landed on the ground, they barked and then went chasing after the fallen cats.

More cats and dogs were falling all over the little town of Oakmont. Nobody, except old Johnny Blake, knew what was going on.

"Why, it's raining cats and dogs," old Johnny Blake cackled. "Just like the old days."

Meanwhile, a huge number of cats and dogs were now running through the streets of Oakmont. They were all of different breeds and colors and they kept falling out of the sky.

The children of Oakmont were extremely happy. "Can we keep him?" little Eddie Winkle asked his parents upon seeing a collie fall from the sky and run across their front lawn.

"Oh, a little cat," said little Emma Woodward, seeing a Siamese cat fall from the sky. "I think she must be hungry."

They were hungry all right. More cats and dogs kept falling from the sky as the others chased each other or searched for food. In fact, cats and dogs were falling all over the town. They landed on cars, people and houses. And they kept falling.

"Just like the old days," laughed old Johnny Blake. "Cats and dogs all over the place."

People, however, became scared as the cats and dogs ran through the streets of town. No one knew if these were wild creatures or not. Some landed on people's heads and backs.

"Can we keep them?" the children kept asking their parents.

Some people decided to let the cats and dogs in their houses. They were good pets for free, the people decided, and they fed them and named them and let them sleep in the living room.

More and more cats and dogs of various shapes and sizes and color combinations fell from the sky until there were thousands running through the streets of Oakmont.

No one knew what to do about the situation. Cats and dogs were running everywhere. Then, suddenly, they stopped falling.

"What a storm," cackled old Johnny Blake. "This is one for the record books."

As the clouds moved to the south and the sun appeared once again, everyone could see that the town was now filled with cats and dogs. So many cats and dogs.

"We'll sell them and collect some money for the town," said the mayor. "People will come from all over the country to see Oakmont's variety of cats and dogs."

And that's just what they did. They advertised the cats and dogs on the internet and television and soon people were coming from other towns and cities to look at the Oakmont pet collection.

Many people of Oakmont adopted some of the cats and dogs that fell from the sky and let the town sell all the thousands of others. It took years before all the cats and dogs were finally sold. In all that time, there was not one robbery in Oakmont. The mice were all gone from the town, too. Stories of the odd storm spread across the land.

"They don't have storms like that anymore," laughed old Johnny Blake. "That was sure one for the records."

And it was, too. It was the only time in the history of the world that it actually rained cats and dogs. Not many believe it, but it happened. Just ask old Johnny Blake.

The Longest Fart

It began one winter night. Old Man Haggle had been left alone by his wife to visit a sick friend. When it came time to eat supper, Old Man Haggle decided he would make chili and corned beef and cabbage. He thought he could make the food without much of a fuss, but soon he discovered it was more difficult than he thought.

He added a lot of spices, and finally, decided the meal was ready to be eaten. He put the chili in a bowl and the corned beef and cabbage on a plate and he began to eat.

"Tastes pretty good if I do say so myself," he remarked, after tasting the chili. "Just as good as Louise makes it."

He was finishing the corned beef and cabbage and the last of the chili when it first started. It began as a high note like that from a bugle and echoed through the tiny house.

"Maybe too many spices," he said to himself as the foul gas wafted through the air.

But the fart didn't end. No, it began sounding like a trumpet doing the scales, up and down and up and down, high and low and high and low, as the stench filled the house.

"Geez, I better open the windows," Old Man Haggle said to himself as the noisy fart continued. "Louise would faint if she were here."

So he opened the windows, and the stench of the continuing fart poured into the outside air. A stray cat walking along suddenly sniffed the air and jumped ten feet backwards. He then dashed down the street looking for some place to hide.

Meanwhile, the fart continued. Old Man Haggle tried walking around, hoping that would end it. It didn't. He tried drinking water, hoping that would put out the fire in his belly. It didn't. He thought of going outside until it was over, but the noise was louder than ever.

"That's what I get fooling around with pots and pans," he said to himself. "Wait until Louise comes back, I'll really be in trouble."

The fart continued. It was now ten minutes, fifteen minutes, twenty minutes and onward since there was peace and breathable air. Old Man Haggle didn't know what to do. The gas filled up the house with the most awful odor ever known to mankind.

Old Man Haggle thought he was going to die. He was thinking what his tombstone would say when there was a knock on the door.

He threw open the door and the man standing in the doorway began to gag.

"Help me!" Old Man Haggle shouted as the fart sung in a high, shrill note and the gas soured the air.

The man began to run from Old Man Haggle's door upon smelling the billowing gas. A dog next door began to howl. Three birds sitting in a nearby tree fell to the ground stone-cold dead.

"Wait!" Old Man Haggle shouted. "It wasn't me, I didn't do it!"

One could barely hear the words amid the loud singing of his ass. The noise continued throughout the night. Old Man Haggle had a hard time trying to get to sleep. Every time he was about to fall asleep, the fart hit an unusually high note.

In the morning, he was tired and couldn't bear to smell the air any longer. "It isn't that bad," he tried telling himself. "After all, it is mine and I should be used to it."

The fart continued throughout the day. The sound kept changing from high to low, but it rippled through the air without stopping.

"Let's see who holds the record?" Old Man Haggle said to himself, picking up his phone. "Bernard Clemmens from London. Two minutes, 42 seconds. Well, I definitely have that record beat. Beat by a mile."

Later that day, Old Man Haggle was still farting. It had already been two days of sustained flatulence. He hadn't been to the bathroom in all that time and wondered why he did not get the necessary feeling.

As a particularly nasty smell flooded the room, Old Man Haggle heard the front door open.

"Jimmy?"

It was Louise! He shuffled into the front room and there lying by the open door was Louise – she had fainted dead away.

"It wasn't me," Old Man Haggle tried to explain. "It was the crickets. Can't you hear them? I've been stepping on them all day."

"Crickets?" Louise muttered. "They must be in your pants because I hear them singing still, you old dog."

Louise eventually got up and turned on all the fans in the house. She then put a clip on her nose and waited for Old Man Haggle to stop farting.

But the farting didn't stop. Two days, three days, four days and five. No one came near the Haggle house. Anyone who did immediately caught a whiff of the horrid air and ran away. Louise was thinking of going to a hotel without Old Man Haggle when the fart suddenly stopped. All that was left was the most horrible stench one would ever smell on this planet.

"Well, what's for dinner?" Old Man Haggle asked as there was silence in the house once more.

"Dinner?" Louise said. "How can you even think of food right now?"

They opened the windows, they kept the fans running, and slowly, the air began to clear.

"Well, I beat the record," Old Man Haggle said. "Five days, six hours, 16 minutes and 23 seconds."

"I think we'll eat oatmeal tonight," Louise said.

They were sitting there eating at the kitchen table when Old Man Haggle sat back and smiled. He suddenly burped. The burp continued for minutes and then hours.

"Here we go again," Louise said. "Another world record."

Old Man Haggle's burp ended later that night. It lasted eight hours, 12 minutes, and upon breathing normally once again, Old Man Haggle resolved he would never eat again.

Goody Goody

Goody Goody was always very good. She was always nice to everybody and tried not to hate anyone.

People smiled whenever Goody Goody came near. The children loved her not only because she was so nice to them, but because she always had a positive thing to say.

"How's everything?" one of the children would ask.

"Nice and sunny," Goody Goody would reply.

Then she would buy one of them a vanilla ice cream cone and smile. "It's a good day to sing," she would say in a merry voice.

The only one who didn't like Goody Goody was Jim Crow. Now he was a mean one, Jim Crow, if you know what I mean. Yes, he was as evil as Goody Goody was nice. Jim Crow didn't like anyone, he hated everybody, and he especially hated Goody Goody.

One day, he saw her coming down the street and decided to begin hurting the children playing nearby.

"You can't play with him, he's different from you," Jim Crow sneered as he pushed one of the children away.

The child began to cry. Goody Goody saw this and she walked over to Jim Crow.

"Trying to make it rain on a nice, sunny day?" she asked.

"What are you going to do about it?" frowned Jim Crow.

"Anything I am able to do," she replied.

"Well, do your best, mamby pamby, because it's not going to be enough," Jim Crow sneered.

Goody Goody smiled and then took the crying child's hand. "Everything will be hunky dory if you just listen to the breeze," she said.

The child smiled. "I can't seem to understand what he's saying," he explained.

"Well, he's telling you that if you can understand him, then you would be a daffodil," she said.

"Well, I'm not a daffodil," the child said.

"No, and if you understood mean people like Jim Crow, you would be a bigot," she explained.

"What's a bigot?" the child wanted to know.

"Why someone who laughs when the thunder frightens and smiles when the rain spoils a perfectly nice, sunny day," she said.

"I don't like bigots," the child said.

"No, you really shouldn't," Goody Goody said. "They like to spoil everyone's nice, sunny day with their words of hate and their senseless acts of violence."

"It's not good to hate," the child said.

Goody Goody smiled. "You're so right, my young friend," she laughed. "Hating is for people who aren't very bright and always want blood to fall from the sky."

The child smiled, and then the other children grabbed each other's hands and began to sing.

"It's a Rainbow World!" they sang.

Jim Crow heard the singing and got very upset. "Stop that annoying singing," he growled. "You're not supposed to be getting along with each other."

"But we are warm and happy," Goody Goody replied.

"Well, that's going to end," Jim Crow snarled. "When I get through with you, you'll all hate each other."

"But it's not good to hate," said one of the children.

"That's perfectly sunny," Goody Goody said. "There's too much hating in the world and not enough liking. I choose to like before I hate, not hate before I like. Who's with me?"

The children gathered around Goody Goody and then more children came from other neighborhoods and then more older kids came to see what was going on.

"People are annoying," Jim Crow grumbled. "It is so much more enjoyable fighting with someone and excluding them from doing something than being friends with them and listening to their annoying happiness."

"We have been fighting long enough," Goody Goody said. "It's now time to see what things would be like if people actually liked each other. If we lived together without hate and prejudice, the world would be a better place."

"No, no, don't listen to that cream puff," Jim Crow snarled. "It's impossible for people to live with each other without fighting and arguing. Impossible!"

"No, it's not impossible!" shouted Goody Goody. "Think positively and turn all negatives to positives. Then you'll see that a warm, sunny day is always better than a dark, dreary rainstorm."

The people listened and began thinking positively.

"May I assist you in your efforts?" someone asked someone else.

"A nice sunny day it is," someone else said.

"No point in arguing, there's always an agreeable solution to be found," another person said.

Soon, all the people were seeing the positive side of a situation and thinking optimistically instead of pessimistically and negatively. Jim Crow couldn't believe it and got very angry.

"No, hit him in the stomach and make him see your point," he growled. "Knock your neighbor down and then kick him in the ribs."

But the people didn't listen to Jim Crow and soon they were hugging and kissing each other.

"Very nice to know you," someone said.

"Yes, everyone is a rainbow," another person said.

Goody Goody was very happy when she saw what was happening. She smiled and began to sing in a merry voice of joy.

"It's a Rainbow World!" she sang.

People joined in and they made a big circle and danced and laughed through the day. Goody Goody looked for Jim Crow, but couldn't find him anywhere. He had obviously given up.

"Peace is not impossible!" shouted Goody Goody.

The people shouted and danced in reply and Goody Goody hoped that Jim Crow and his prejudice and hate had gone for good.

The Pumpkinman

*H*ave you ever seen the Pumpkinman?
They say he appears every Halloween when the air is crisp and the wind blows in from the north. He is usually dressed in black, they say, from head to toe, and he emerges from a nearby pumpkin patch as soon as the sun goes down on Halloween. No one knows who he is or where he came from, but according to the ancient Celtic people, it was on Halloween that the spirit world could walk among the living.

Have you ever seen the Pumpkinman?

I first saw the Pumpkinman on Halloween a few years ago. At least, I thought it was the Pumpkinman. I had heard that he came back every year from out of the pumpkin patch because he was upset that people were taking over his land. *His* land, mind you.

Anyway, my friend, Matt, and I decided to wait for him one Halloween at the entrance of the old pumpkin patch near our homes. The land was once part of a huge farm, and many said it was once owned by the Pumpkinman himself. So we sat on the old white fence that surrounded the pumpkin patch and waited. And waited.

Matt and I were wearing our Halloween costumes just in case something happened. I was a Devil, and Matt was a Pirate. We figured if we couldn't, at least, scare the Pumpkinman, we would be able to escape without him ever seeing our faces. So we put our masks on, and just waited there on the fence.

After the sun went down, it got pretty spooky. There were big black crows flying around, and the wind began to howl. Matt and I were getting pretty nervous, but the Pumpkinman never did show up. We waited as long as we could, and then we decided we would go trick or treating, collect as much candy as we could, and then come back and wait some more.

As we reached the neighborhood near our homes, we saw all the other kids in their Halloween costumes. Their bags were already half-full with candy and all kinds of other delicious treats. Matt and I began knocking on doors, trying to catch up.

Our bags were soon almost filled with some of the best candy you could think of. Somebody was even handing out candy apples! I wondered if my mother would allow me to eat it, I mean with all the stories you hear about how unsafe it is to eat anything that isn't wrapped. Anyway, I was happy just to look at it. The light of the moon glowed on the red candy coating. I never had seen anything so delicious in all my life!

But we weren't finished trick or treating. So I placed the candy apple inside my bag, and we continued on. When we reached the houses down the street, we noticed a tall kid, wearing black with a Jack-o-lantern mask, trick or treating with the other kids. He looked like he was enjoying himself, stuffing candy in his pockets, and using what looked like a handkerchief to collect even more of the loot. There was a glowing light inside his pumpkin mask, and I wondered how he was able to create such a cool effect.

Anyway, we trick or treated a bit longer, and then when all of our bags were filled we gathered on the sidewalk and began to laugh. One by one, we began taking off our masks.

"Oh, it's you, Ashley," I said, as one of the Princesses took off her mask. "Can you believe how much candy we got?"

"Oh, we had even more last year!" she replied. "But I guess this is a pretty good haul."

Then Matt and I took off our masks, and we all stood there looking into each other's bags at all the candy we had collected. It was then I noticed once again the tall kid in the Jack-o-lantern mask. "That's a pretty cool costume," I told him. "But aren't you hot in there?"

He nodded his head, the light still glowing inside.

"Why don't you take it off?" I asked. "You'll probably feel much better."

He looked at me, and then reached up with both hands, black gloves on each, and began pulling at the pumpkin mask. The kids began laughing, thinking he was having so much trouble taking it off. And then it happened!

He tugged on the Pumpkin mask until suddenly, the entire Pumpkin head popped off his neck! All of us looked at him with our mouths open as he held the Pumpkin head in his hands, the light still glowing inside.

Then the girls began to scream, and all of us began running away. I looked back, and could see he had put the Pumpkin head back onto his neck! He was bending down and grabbing our trick or treat bags! We had left all our candy behind!

"Hey, he's stealing our candy!" I shouted. "He can't get away from all of us!"

Some of the girls refused to listen, and kept running in the other direction, but many of us began chasing him through the night, a full moon glowing overhead. You couldn't believe how fast he ran, although his arms were filled with all of our Halloween candy!

"Stop, you thief!" we shouted.

He kept running faster and faster, until he ran so fast his pumpkin head flew right off his neck! We watched as the big orange head fell to the ground! Many of the kids began running away, but Matt and I kept following him.

"He won't get far now!" I said to Matt.

But like by some miracle, he just kept running. He was still carrying all our Halloween candy, and he kept running faster and faster towards the old pumpkin patch. There wasn't any way we would ever be able to catch him. But when he finally reached the pumpkin patch, he stopped running and put all the Halloween candy down on the grass.

Matt and I were thinking about stealing all of it back when we watched as he reached down and picked up a pumpkin. He held it in his gloved hands for a moment, and then shifting it to the left hand, began poking holes in it with his right! There were soon two eyes, a nose, and a mouth. Then he lifted the pumpkin up, and placed it on his neck!

Then he bent down, gathered all the Halloween candy, and disappeared into the old pumpkin patch. Matt and I just looked at each other, and shook our heads.

"No way I'm going in there tonight," said Matt.

I agreed. It was just too dark and scary in there. And there was no way I was going to let him get us, as well as the Halloween candy.

I looked at Matt with my eyes wide open. "It was him, for sure," I finally said. "The Pumpkinman!"

Matt and I walked home that night without any Halloween candy. Our parents asked us what had happened, but we didn't tell them anything. They probably wouldn't have believed us, anyway! And even if they had, there was little they could do about it. That pumpkin patch was dark, and the Pumpkinman could have hidden anywhere he wanted.

The next morning, Matt and I went back to the old pumpkin patch. Halloween was now over, but we wanted to see if we could find any sign that what we saw was not something created by the night. We stepped inside the old pumpkin patch, and what do you think we saw?

Well, right there on the ground was a half-eaten candy apple! My candy apple!

We left the old pumpkin patch, and then walked up the street. There on the ground was a smashed pumpkin head! The same pumpkin head that had flown off the Pumpkinman's neck!

But no one ever really believed us. They said the Pumpkinman was all a product of our imagination. Still, Matt and I know what we saw, and to this day, we truly believe we saw the Pumpkinman.

Have you ever seen the Pumpkinman?

Well, my advice to you is run for your life if you ever do because he'll get you for sure! You and your Halloween candy, and that's no lie!

Nightingale

Once there was a beautiful girl who was known as Nightingale because she had the most beautiful singing voice in the entire world. She lived in a small house in a small village with her half-sister and her parents. Her half-sister was very jealous of Nightingale's beautiful singing voice, and since she was older by two years, could order her little half-sister to do anything she wanted.

After ordering her to clean the floor and the dishes, her half-sister had an idea. "Nightingale," she said, "since I am two years older, you will do as I say. I've decided I want to meet that handsome prince and you will help me. You will hide in the bushes, and then I will pretend to sing to him, and you will be my singing voice."

Nightingale knew she could not refuse her older half-sister, and nodded her head. "Yes, Tarisa, I understand," she said. "I will be your singing voice when you go to the handsome prince."

Tarisa, the older half-sister, smiled. "Remember, you are not to be seen," she warned her. "Just sit behind the bushes and sing a beautiful song."

Later that day, Tarisa led Nightingale to the prince's castle. When she spotted the handsome prince in one of the windows, she told Nightingale to hide in the bushes. Then she ordered Nightingale to sing.

"Here I am for you," sang Nightingale. "There you are for me. Together we will be. In the end, you'll see. I love you."

It was the most beautiful song anyone had ever heard. The handsome prince ran to the window to see who was singing the beautiful song. He spotted Tarisa down below with her arms in the air and her mouth open.

"Are you the one singing that beautiful song?" asked the handsome prince.

"Why, yes," replied Tarisa. "Are you pleased?"

"Yes, very much," answered the prince. "Why don't you come inside?"

Tarisa, however, was afraid to go inside the castle without Nightingale. What if he should want me to sing to everyone?"

"I'm afraid I can't," she finally replied. "I can only sing out in the fresh air."

"Very well," said the prince. "I will come out to you."

The handsome prince emerged from the castle, and walked over to Tarisa, who was still standing in front. He looked at her and noticed she wasn't as beautiful as he had hoped. But that will not stop me, he said to himself, if she can sing so well.

So the prince sat down in front of Tarisa and asked her to sing. "If you wish," she replied, nodding to Nightingale, who was still hiding in the bushes.

"Here I am for you," sang Nightingale. "There you are for me. Together we will be. In the end, you'll see. I love you."

When Tarisa closed her mouth and put down her arms, the prince stood and applauded. "You have the most beautiful voice I have ever heard," he said. "In honor of your gift, I will hold a singing contest and the one who wins shall be my princess."

Tarisa smiled. "It will be my pleasure," she said.

Then the prince walked over and kissed Tarisa. "The contest shall begin tomorrow," he said. "There is no one who can win but you."

The prince smiled, and then walked back to the castle. "See you tomorrow," he said, disappearing inside.

As the castle door closed, Tarisa turned to Nightingale with a laugh. "Did you hear what he said?" she asked. "If we win the singing contest, I will marry the prince."

Nightingale didn't feel very good about helping Tarisa to marry the handsome prince, but she decided there was nothing she could do about it.

The day of the contest, Tarisa wore her best pink dress and made Nightingale wear black. "Now you will stand in the back of the stage behind the scenery," she told Nightingale. "And don't let anybody see you singing or I'll tell them you were trying to ruin the contest and they'll lock you up in the tower for sure."

Nightingale nodded her head, deciding there was really nothing else she could do. Then the two of them walked off to the castle.

When they reached the castle, they saw a huge stage had been set up in front. The background scenery was that of a blue sky.

"Now you go behind that blue sky scenery," Tarisa told Nightingale. "And, remember, don't get caught."

Nightingale made her way quietly behind the scenery. There she met an old dwarf who was in charge of keeping the scenery up.

"Why are you back here?" the old dwarf wondered. "All the contestants are supposed to gather in front."

"But I'm not in the contest," said Nightingale. "I'm only supposed to make sure no one ruins the contest from behind the scenery."

The old dwarf nodded. "Okay," he grumbled, "but don't get in my way."

Nightingale went to the side of the stage and peeked out from behind the scenery. The contest was a huge affair with many contestants set to sing. Three judges sat in front below the stage, and the line of contestants stretched down the center aisle. Tarisa was fourth in line.

One by one the contestants sang for the judges. When it was Tarisa's turn, she walked slowly across the stage towards where the judges were seated.

"Sing, Nightingale, sing!" she whispered.

"Here I am for you," sang Nightingale from behind the scenery. "There you are for me. Together we will be. In the end, you'll see. I love you."

When Tarisa closed her mouth and put down her arms, everyone cheered and applauded. It was the most beautiful voice they had ever heard. The judges immediately voted her into the final round.

Meanwhile, behind the scenery, the old dwarf looked suspiciously at Nightingale when she began to sing.

"You sing very well," he grumbled. "But I doubt anyone heard you."

Then Nightingale peeked out from behind the scenery once again. Tarisa was now in the final singing round with three other girls and one boy. They stood before the judges ready to sing.

It was at this moment that the old dwarf walked over to Nightingale carrying a glass of water. "You look thirsty," he said. "Drink this and your voice will be crystal clear."

So Nightingale drank the water and fell into a deep sleep. "This sleeping potion will allow me to find out what really is going on," laughed the old dwarf.

When it was Tarisa's turn to sing, she turned towards the scenery for a moment. "Sing, Nightingale, sing!" she whispered.

But, this time, she heard nothing.

"Sing, Nightingale, sing!" she whispered once again.

Again she heard nothing.

Tarisa then tried to sing without Nightingale. She made horrid, squeaky sounds and everyone began to laugh. Tarisa stood there quite angry, telling herself she would get even with Nightingale for embarrassing her in front of the whole village, when she suddenly turned into a croaking toad.

Behind the scenery, the old dwarf laughed. Then he looked at the sleeping Nightingale, walked over, and kissed her on the lips.

Nightingale opened her eyes and saw the old dwarf change into the handsome prince. "You knew all along?" she asked.

The handsome prince nodded his head. "The king's sorcerer changed me into an old dwarf," he said. "Then he promised to change your half-sister into a squawking toad if she couldn't sing on her own."

Nightingale smiled.

"Now it is your turn to sing, Nightingale," said the handsome prince. "And become my princess. Sing, Nightingale, sing!"

So Nightingale sang for the judges and the crowd and everyone agreed she had the most beautiful voice they had ever heard. They immediately proclaimed her the winner of the singing contest and the handsome prince's bride.

Nightingale and the handsome prince were soon married and Nightingale sang to him all the time. Everyone agreed she had the most beautiful singing voice in all the world and was as beautiful as her voice and they lived happily ever after.

Johnny Flakes

ohnny Flakes became real one frosty Christmas day.

Snow had fallen on Christmas Eve. On Christmas morning, out came the children, and they laughed and flopped around. Soon Jimmy and Emily began making snow angels. And what fine snow angels they were.

Jimmy was lying in the snow, moving his arms back and forth. Before too long his angel had wings.

Emily was also lying in the snow, moving her arms back and forth. Soon her angel had wings, too.

Then Jimmy moved his legs back and forth through the snow. Now his angel had wings and a gown.

Emily did the same with her legs. After moving them back and forth in the snow, her angel had wings and a gown.

Jimmy watched as Emily stood up and began running through the snow. "Aren't you going to say a prayer?" he asked.

"What for?" laughed Emily.

"But this is Christmas snow," said Jimmy. "If you say a prayer in Christmas snow, then it's sure to be granted."

"Silly boy," Emily said with a smile.

"You just watch," said Jimmy. "I'm going to say a prayer to make my snow angel come alive."

All the children started laughing, but Jimmy didn't care. He made his wish in Christmas snow and then hoped for the best.

"Bless my snow angel," he said. "Amen."

Jimmy stood up and looked around. And there, floating in the air, was a real live snow angel wearing white. He looked very much like Jimmy, except he had white hair and a golden halo.

"I'm Johnny Flakes," the snow angel said. "And I'll grant you any wish you like."

That's how Johnny Flakes came alive that bright, cold Christmas.

The children could not believe that Johnny Flakes was real. "But this is Christmas snow," Jimmy explained.

The children had a great time with Johnny Flakes. He carried their sleds though the air and then took each of them on a trip of their very own.

Jimmy, however, still didn't know what he would wish for. He thought of many things – motorized cars and computerized robots – but still couldn't decide.

"Maybe you'll decide after I carry you over the ice and snow for a while," said Johnny Flakes.

Jimmy had a great time, but still couldn't decide what to wish for.

"What if you had a wish?" Jimmy asked Johnny Flakes. "What would you wish for?"

"Someone to play with," said Johnny Flakes.

"But you can play with us," said Jimmy. "Don't we have fun?"

"Yes, of course," said Johnny Flakes. "But I do get lonely."

And then Jimmy had an idea. He whispered to Emily and when she heard what he was saying, she smiled.

Then Emily fell back in the snow and began moving her arms back and forth. She then moved her legs back and forth. Before too long, there was an angel with wings and a gown in the snow.

"Bless my snow angel," said Emily. "Amen."

Emily stood up and watched as another snow angel floated into the air. This snow angel was much like Johnny Flakes, except she was slimmer and prettier. She had long, white hair and the prettiest golden halo anyone had ever seen.

"I'm Jenny Flakes," she said. "And I'll grant you any wish you like."

Then Johnny Flakes saw Jenny Flakes and knew the children had made his wish come true.

Jenny Flakes took one look at Johnny Flakes and they were in love. Everyone was happy, especially Jimmy and Emily.

"And now what will your wish be?" asked Johnny Flakes.

"Yes, your wish," said Jenny Flakes.

"Peace on earth and good will among human beings," they laughed. "The happiest of holidays to everyone!"

Todar the Plant-Eating Tiger

There once was a tiger who lived in the Siberian forest in eastern Russia.

His name was Todar. That's Theodore in Russian.

Todar was not an ordinary tiger. You see, he didn't like meat.

Todar ate plants, grass and berries.

He didn't know why he didn't like meat. He just didn't.

He liked sitting in the forest and eating berries.

The other animals were not afraid of Todar. They even liked him.

Sometimes, the other tigers in the forest would laugh at Todar.

"Hey, why don't you eat meat like the rest of us?" a tiger would say.

But Todar wouldn't listen. "Plants and berries are more to my liking," he would reply.

The other tigers would shake their heads and then leave Todar by himself.

But Todar didn't care. He kept right on eating the plants and berries.

One day, human beings came to the forest. They brought with them many cages.

Todar didn't mind. He kept right on eating the plants and berries.

Then one of the humans noticed him. "This one over here is grazing on the grass like a timid sheep."

Before he knew it, the humans put Todar in a small cage. Todar didn't mind. He was still chewing on a mouthful of berries.

The humans carried Todar's cage back to their truck and then put him on a plane.

Before he knew it, he was flying to America. He didn't care, except for the fact that he had run out of berries and plants.

When the plane finally landed, they brought Todar to the zoo. "That's a nice one," the zookeeper said. "But he must be hungry."

Of course, he tried to feed him meat. But Todar would not eat one bite.

"You're going to starve if you don't eat," said the zookeeper. "But it's up to you."

Todar still hadn't eaten when the people came. He just sat there watching them as they stared at him and laughed.

That's when he saw it! A little boy holding an ice cream cone. It doesn't look like meat, Todar thought to himself.

Todar stuck his paw through the bars and grabbed the ice cream cone. The little boy started to cry. That's when the real crying and shouting began!

"That tiger tried to eat my baby!" screamed the little boy's mother. "What a nasty creature!"

But Todar didn't mind. He was busy licking the ice cream cone, which was lying on the floor of his cage.

The zookeeper came running and then saw him licking the ice cream.

"He didn't want to eat your little boy," explained the zookeeper. "He just wanted the ice cream!"

The little boy then looked at Todar and began laughing. "Look, Ma! He's eating my ice cream cone!"

Then all the people stopped crying and shouting and looked at Todar. "He's right!" someone said. "He's eating the ice cream."

They all began to laugh and moved closer to Todar's cage. "Why, that tiger is eating ice cream!" someone shouted.

Todar's cage was soon surrounded by a large crowd of people.

"Maybe he also likes chocolate," a little girl said. She threw her chocolate bar into Todar's cage.

Todar licked his lips and began eating the chocolate. It tasted better than anything he had ever tasted in his entire life.

"See, mother, he likes chocolate," the little girl said. And then the entire crowd began to laugh.

The zookeeper finally saw what was going on and had the strangest idea. "Maybe this tiger doesn't like to eat meat," he said to himself.

The very next day, the zookeeper left a bowl of oatmeal in Todar's cage. Todar smelled it, and then began eating it until there was nothing left.

The zookeeper smiled, and then gave Todar a piece of chocolate. Todar licked his lips and ate it in one gulp.

And that's how the zookeeper discovered that Todar liked to eat plants and berries and things like that.

Soon they put a sign outside of Todar's cage. It said, "Todar the Plant-Eating Tiger."

When the people saw the sign, they all laughed. A little girl threw a flower into Todar's cage. He sniffed at it and then ate it!

And he was very happy.

When Pigs Fly

Whenever someone expected something incredible to happen, people would always say it would happen when pigs could fly.

"There will be peace in the world," Elmo Hatcher was saying.

"When pigs can fly," replied Wally Jones.

"Everyone will be equal and everyone will be free," Elmo continued.

"When pigs can fly," answered Wally.

"There will be no more wars and man and woman will live together in utter happiness."

"When pigs can fly."

They were standing there by the barn, looking up in the clear, blue sky, when a fat, pink pig with wings flew over the house.

"Did you see that, Wally?"

"See what, Elmo?"

"A pig with wings flying over the house."

Wally smiled. "Oh, sure, pigs flying," he replied.

"But that's exactly what I'm trying to tell you, Wally," Elmo said.

"Tell me what?"

"That a pig was flying."

Wally began to laugh. "You sure are funny, Elmo," he said.

"Not trying to be funny."

"A pig flying," Wally laughed. "That will happen when pigs can fly."

"But I saw one flying over the house," Elmo explained.

"You been drinking that homemade moonshine again, Elmo."

"Why, there he is right now flying over the pasture."

Wally looked and gasped.

"Is that what I think it is, Elmo?"

"Just like I told you, Wally."

In the distance, one could clearly see a big, fat, pink pig with wings flying over the cow pasture.

Wally looked at Elmo and sighed. "Only one, Elmo, nothing to get excited about," he said.

"Only one?"

"Yeah, things will happen when pigs can fly, Elmo. Plural, understand? That's only one pig."

"You ever see a pig with wings before?"

"No, but it's possible."

"Oh, it is, is it?"

Just then, Elmo glimpsed another big, fat, pink pig with wings flying over the house.

"Well, you can get ready for the end, Wally, I just seen another one fly away into the sky."

"Can't be," Wally answered.

"But they are flying, Wally."

"But it's impossible."

"Nothing is impossible, Wally."

"But where did they get the wings?" he asked.

"Don't know, maybe God."

"What does God care about pigs?"

"He loves all creatures, don't you know that?"

Wally looked up and spotted the second pig with wings flying over the pasture.

"I see it but I don't believe it," he said.

Then from behind the barn another big, fat, pink pig took off into the sky.

"There's another one, Wally."

"Another pig with wings?"

"That's what I'm saying."

"Well, why does the Lord want to go and do a thing like that?"

"Maybe to prove nothing is impossible," Elmo explained. "All you need is confidence and a belief that everything is possible and then, everything becomes possible."

Wally and Elmo stood there and watched as two more pigs flew over the house.

"Well, pigs are flying all right," Wally said.

"That's what I've been saying," Elmo said.

Before too long, there were hundreds and then thousands of pigs with wings flying through the air.

"Truly a miracle," Elmo said.

"If that's what you're really into," Wally said.

They watched as the big, fat, pink pigs with wings flew away over the cow pasture.

"Well, you think there will be peace in the world?" Elmo asked.

Wally thought for a moment and frowned. "When elephants parachute from the heavens," he said.

"Well, pigs are flying, Wally, anything is possible."

"Giving pigs wings is nothing special," Wally explained. "Now having elephants parachute from the heavens, that would be something to stop and marvel at."

"Some folks can never be pleased," Elmo said with a shake of his head.

Up above, thousands of big, fat, pink pigs with wings were flying towards the west. Elmo squinted into the fading light searching for a parachute and something huge underneath knowing anything was possible in this world.

Thousands and thousands of pigs were, meanwhile, flying over the hushed landscape.

The Boy Who Hated Muhammad

There was a boy who hated the prophet Muhammad. He hated him because Muhammad and his followers hated anyone who didn't believe the way they did. There were stories told to the boy about Muhammad lusting after many women and abusing children who were just about his age. Anyone who didn't agree with Muhammad was called an infidel and deserved death. The boy didn't like this attitude.

So the boy began drawing pictures of Muhammad. They were pictures of Muhammad shouting and killing. The boy hung the pictures outside and the birds and animals attacked them and tore them to pieces.

"He didn't like women," the boy would say to anyone who would listen. "He didn't like children."

The boy kept drawing the pictures of Muhammad and he began hanging them up all over his room. There were pictures of Muhammad growling and hating and praying to Allah, who was the God he thought would destroy all non-believers.

Instead, the boy decided he would destroy Allah. So he drew pictures of Allah and began destroying them by burning them or tearing them up or letting the dog rip them up into tiny, jagged pieces. Nothing ever happened to the boy when he did this and so, he decided Allah was a joke and didn't exist.

He knew if the followers of Muhammad and Allah ever found out what he was doing, they would try to hurt him or kill him. The boy didn't care. He couldn't help hating Muhammad and Allah.

They hated America and Israel and anyone who thought what they were doing was disgusting, the boy said to himself. He knew they had burned American flags and Israeli flags and had urged their people to do violence against the rest of the world.

The boy who hated Muhammad decided to burn all his pictures of the prophet. He placed them in the fireplace and burned them along with a rotting log. He burned all the pictures of Muhammad and all the pictures of Allah and decided he would no longer think about such things.

It was many days later that he was looking through one of his drawers and found one of the drawings of Muhammad and Allah. They were angry and shaking hands and grinning about all the dead bodies they were standing on. There were hundreds of dead bodies underneath them and the bodies and blood covered the ground.

The boy took the picture outside and placed it on the grass. Then he took a firecracker and placed it underneath the picture. Lighting the firecracker, he blew up the picture into little pieces. They fluttered in the air and sailed into the sky. That's the last he would ever see of Muhammad and Allah, the boy told himself.

Years later, he came across a picture of Muhammad in a green and yellow sheet. Muhammad was angry and telling everyone to hate outsiders or infidels and wage a holy war against the world. The boy began hating Muhammad once again.

He took the picture of Muhammad and began shooting at it with his bb gun. When the picture was full of holes, he took it to the hillside and burned it. He knew the followers of Muhammad would kill him if they knew what he had done. He didn't care. He decided he would speak to God about it.

So the boy went to a nearby hill and looked up into the sky. "Do you think I did the right thing?" he asked.

There was a crackling of lightning and a blast of thunder and then the boy heard a voice sizzling in the sky. "You have done well," the voice said. "These people do not represent a good and peaceful Lord."

The boy smiled. "Will you prevent them from harming me?" he asked.

"I will do all that I can do," said the voice. "You must be responsible for your actions, however."

"Yes, I guess that is true," he mumbled. "I will continue to pray to you and do what you think is best."

"Try not to hate," the voice said. "But be disgusted with that which you know is wrong and violent."

The boy listened to the voice soaring in the wind and began to do a little dance. "Yes, the Lord knows that I'm right to hate those that hate and kill," he said. "They represent the evil of the world, not the Lord's true wishes."

The boy listened again for the voice in the sky, but it had disappeared. He was alone standing there on the top of the hill. He looked into the clear, blue sky and laughed.

"I am glad the Lord is with me," he shouted into the sky. "I love the Lord and hate all those who defy Him."

He then walked slowly down the hillside, looking up into the sky, and shouted, "Amen."